BOOK 1

To GRANT
& Seth -

Believe in Aliens!

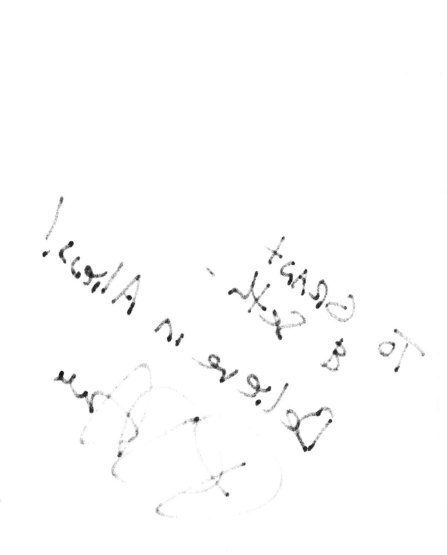

BOOK 1

by
CONNOR HOOVER

Alien Treasure Hunters Book 1

Copyright © 2018 by Connor Hoover.
All rights reserved.

www.connorhoover.com

Paperback ISBN: 978-1985237346

For Zach, for showing me how to be
adventurous

CHAPTER 1

Colton tossed the baseball up again, catching it behind his back, like that might make it more of a challenge. This had to be the fiftieth time he'd caught it. Maybe the hundredth. Why couldn't he have gone to summer camp like his friends? The next few weeks were going to be the worst. Besides practicing baseball—all by himself—there wasn't a single thing he could figure out to do. Day two of summer break, and he already wanted to die of boredom.

Whatever. Up the baseball went again. And again. And again. This was way too easy. Maybe he should have let his little brother Tyler play with him. Maybe tomorrow he would. Or maybe not, because how cool was it to spend your summer break hanging out with your little brother?

Colton got ready to throw, but this time, instead of tossing the ball upward, he threw it forward, toward the green wooden fence. The second it left his hand, he ran as fast as he could. He would beat the ball and get there first. Except two things went completely wrong. First, instead of him catching the ball before it hit the fence, it sailed over the fence and out of sight. And second, because Colton was so busy looking at the ball, he didn't stop in time and slammed into the fence.

He fell to the hard dirt ground and lay on his back, looking up at the blue sky. But the sun was so bright, he had to squint and look away. It was always bright here in Roswell, New Mexico. Bright and boring.

"Let's pretend that didn't happen," Colton said to himself since no one else was around. He stood up, ignoring the stars that floated through his vision, and brushed the dirt off his jeans and t-shirt. Running into the fence wasn't the smoothest thing he'd ever done in his life. A quick glance around told him that no one was here to see it. That was good. His friends would have made so much fun of him.

Colton glanced left and right, looking for a way in, but there was no gate that he could see. He was going to have to go over.

He jumped up, catching the top of the green fence with his fingers. His feet slammed into the wood. That's when he heard the growling.

Uh oh. That couldn't be good.

He swung his legs and caught one foot on the top of the fence and then pulled his body up so he could see over. And then he wished he hadn't. On the other side of the fence was the Roswell Junkyard. It had been here for as long as he'd been alive. Maybe it had even been here forever, since the time of the dinosaurs, and there were dinosaur bones buried under all those cars. But the junkyard wasn't the bad part. The bad part was that staring right at Colton was a giant brown dog with his baseball in its huge mouth.

The dog growled the second it saw Colton and lowered the front of its body like it was preparing to pounce. This was the worst possible scenario Colton could imagine. Then the dog growled one final time and took off running, still holding the baseball in its mouth.

"Get back here!" Colton called.

The dog didn't listen. Or at least didn't obey. It only ran deeper into the junkyard until it disappeared out of sight.

"You have got to be kidding me!" Colton said, dropping inside the fence. He had to get the baseball. It was the last one he had. He'd lost—or destroyed— five more in the past month. There was no way his dad would buy him any more. And since Colton had zero money, if he ever wanted to throw the baseball again this entire summer, he was going to have to get the ball back.

Colton followed the path the monster dog had taken while also trying not to step on all the junk around him. Whoever came up with the name junkyard, was master of the obvious. This place had junk. All kinds of junk. Sure, there was the normal junk, like tires and old cars and stuff like that, but there were also old computers and televisions and stoves and refrigerators. A person could live here and have everything they needed for a long, happy life.

Wait. That was a horrible thought. What if a person really did live out here and reported Colton for trespassing. He could get arrested and go to jail. His dad would explode with anger.

He'd get the ball and leave. It would be as simple as that.

The junkyard was huge, like as big as the cheesy Roswell carnival they'd been to earlier in the spring. It would have been impossible to find the dog in this place except that there was a nice path that led through all the stacks of junk. Colton kept to the path, because the dog must have also, unless it could jump over piles of old cars.

Maybe it could. It was big enough. It probably ate cars for dinner. And baseballs.

Colton stopped the second he heard the growling. Fear filled him, but he pushed it away. He wasn't scared of some dog.

Okay, fine, maybe he was. But only this dog. This dog was a monster. It was fear-worthy. But he'd never admit that to his friends. It would be like running into the fence. Everyone would laugh at him.

Colton straightened his shoulders and walked forward, turning the corner to where he knew the dog would be waiting. And sure enough, there it was, baseball at its feet, drool spilling from its hideous mouth. Each of its paws was easily as big as the baseball, and it could have chewed up his baseball glove in seconds.

5

The dog looked directly at Colton and let out a bark that made Colton's ears ring. Then it let out another bark and ran off, leaving the ball behind.

Perfect!

Colton ran forward, ready to grab the baseball, except he stopped dead in his tracks when someone else crept out from behind a junked car. He recognized her from school—some girl in his grade, but Colton couldn't remember her name.

"You're the one!" she said. "You sent the dog after me!"

Was she crazy?

"Sent the dog after you?" Colton said. "That dog was trying to kill me."

"Kill you?" she said. "It just ran away from you. You probably scared it off with all the noise you were making."

"It stole my baseball," Colton said.

"What? This stupid baseball," the girl said, and kicked it hard, but completely un-athletically, like she'd never kicked a ball before in her life.

The ball bounced off a hubcap and rolled into a nearby car, disappearing from sight.

"Hey!" Colton said, and he darted forward so he could get it. He ducked into the rust bucket, scraping his head. This was not his day.

The car was nothing but a pile of scrap metal, waiting to be crushed. It looked like one of those antique cars, really tall and wide, except the top was sort of dome shaped, like maybe something people drove in the old days—like the 1970s—and thought was cool. Inside, it was pitch black. He could hardly see a thing. He definitely couldn't see the baseball.

"Do you have a flashlight?" Colton called out to the girl. "I can't find it."

She ducked and came in also. "It rolled right inside the door. It couldn't have gone far."

"I know," Colton said. "But it's too dark to see it."

Because the car was so tall and wide, they could both be inside without sitting down and still have a tiny bit of room to move around. Maybe it was a 1970s minivan or something like that. Some of his friend's families had minivans.

"Maybe under here," the girl said, but when she reached down to check under what might have been a seat, two things happened. First, a bunch of lights on the dashboard lit up, making it definitely bright enough to see. Colton immediately saw his baseball and grabbed it. And second, behind them, the door to the minivan/car slammed shut, sealing them inside.

CHAPTER 2

C olton ran to the door and shoved it. It wouldn't budge. And there was no door handle. It had probably fallen off in the last fifty years of sitting in this junkyard.

"Hey . . . um . . . can you help me with this?" he said.

She didn't answer.

He looked back, and there she was, at the dashboard, looking at all the lights and controls and stuff, totally ignoring him.

"Hey, you," he said, since he had no clue what her name was.

This got her attention. She whipped around.

"Do you even know my name?" she said.

Colton wracked his brain trying to remember. They had at least one class together this past year. History, he was pretty sure.

"Of course I do," Colton said. "We had a class together. It's . . ."

"It's Abigail," she said. "And we had three classes together. Science, Language Arts, and History."

He was about to say something along the lines of "We did?" but managed to stop himself since that might seem like he hadn't noticed her in those classes. Which he hadn't. But she didn't need to know that.

"Right," Colton said. "Three classes. And of course your name is Abigail. I'm Colton."

"I know," Abigail said, way too sharply, like she was mad or something.

Wow, she was hard to talk to. And that was saying a lot. Colton could carry on a conversation with a potato.

"Okay, anyway, Abigail, if you could help me with the door, that would be awesome," Colton said. "It's kind of stuck."

"You're probably just not strong enough," Abigail said.

Colton let out a fake laugh. "Yeah, probably not."

He was totally strong enough. He had to be the most athletic kid at school. The door had just slammed really hard.

"Fine," Abigail said, and she was about to help when all of a sudden a bright red light on the dashboard started blinking and a horrible beeping sound blasted through the minivan.

"What did you do?" Colton asked.

"I didn't do anything," Abigail said.

"You must've."

But before she could answer, a voice started talking, really monotone like a recording or something.

"Liftoff in one minute," the voice said. "It is advised that the occupants sit down and fasten their safety belts. It should be noted that liftoff will occur whether the safety belts are fastened or not."

"Did you hear that?" Colton said. Maybe he'd just hit his head too hard on the fence outside the junkyard.

"It must be some kind of joke," Abigail said, and she shoved on the door also.

Together they tried to lift the door or push it outward or anything. But the thing would not budge.

"It's stuck," Abigail said.

"That's what I said," Colton said. "It's stuck."

"Liftoff in thirty seconds," the voice said, and it gave the same safety belt warning as before.

"Try again," Colton said, and they pushed on the door over and over. The whole time the red light blinked and the warning sound beeped and the inside of the car got smaller and smaller, although Colton figured that last part was his imagination.

But he couldn't get the beeping out of his head. It was a countdown. To a liftoff? What did that even mean?

Colton didn't have to wait long to find out.

"Liftoff in five . . . four . . . three . . . two . . . one . . . zero," the voice said.

The car started shaking. More lights flashed on the dashboard. Colton glanced out the front window. The junkyard was getting farther away. Like it was now below them. They were actually in the air, levitating or something like that. Except they were getting farther from the ground with every second that went by.

"Maybe we should sit down?" Abigail said, and she jumped into the seat on the right.

It seemed like a really great idea. Colton plunked his bottom in the chair on the left and fumbled for his seat belt. He barely had it clicked when the car sped up, like a race car, heading directly for outer space.

CHAPTER 3

Colton gripped the armrests of his chair and glanced over at Abigail. "Please tell me this isn't happening."

Unlike him, who felt like they were going to fall out of the sky and to their doom at any second, Abigail had a look on her face like she'd just gotten a new puppy.

"Heck, yeah, this is happening!" she said, and she pressed a bunch of buttons on the dashboard. Or maybe it wasn't really a dashboard. It was more like a control panel . . . for a spaceship!

"I don't think we're in a minivan," Colton said.

"Oh really, genius?" Abigail said. "What gave it away? The Earth disappearing, the blinking red lights, or the fact we're getting closer to the moon with every second that passes?"

He snapped his head back to the window. There was the moon! But it was right in their path. They were going to run into it!

"How do you steer this thing?" Colton said, and he started fumbling with the controls.

Abigail swatted his hands away. "Let me drive. I think I got this."

"You think you got this?" Colton said. "How can you possible 'got this?' We're in a spaceship. Have you ever driven a spaceship before? Have you ever even driven a car before?"

Abigail bit her lip and pressed a button. It turned from blue to yellow. Was that good?

"No," she said. "I've never driven, but I drive with my mom all the time. I'm very observant."

"That's not the same thing!" Colton said.

The moon got closer. They were heading right for it in their spaceship. Spaceship!? That was impossible.

"The steering controls aren't working," Abigail said.

Colton was about to say something about how maybe she just didn't know what she was doing, but he kept his mouth shut. It wasn't like he knew how to drive the thing either.

"I think the controls aren't working," Abigail said.

Terror must've crossed his face, because she immediately said, "But don't panic. I think it's meant to be that way."

"We're supposed to run into the moon?" Colton said. "Who designed this thing anyway?"

"Aliens?" Abigail said. "Or the FBI. It could be either one."

Aliens or the FBI? This was bad and getting worse. All Colton had wanted to do today was play baseball. Now here he was in a spaceship about to crash into the moon.

It really looked like his life was about to end, but then, without any warning, the spaceship jerked to the side, and the moon disappeared from view.

"You did it!" Colton said.

Abigail shook her head. "I didn't do anything. I think—"

There was a loud rumbling noise, like an engine revving up, that drowned out her next words.

"You what?" Colton said.

"I think we're on autopilot," Abigail said.

The revving got louder. The spaceship seemed to hover in space, not moving. And then, like a rubber band snapping, it shot forward, like a bullet. All the stars and planets in the sky became nothing but long streaks of light, zipping by so fast there was no way Colton could tell one from the other.

"Light speed," Abigail said.

"What?" Colton asked.

"I think we're traveling at light speed," she said. "See how everything is moving faster than we can see? That's light speed. We're moving faster than the speed of light."

"People can do that?" Colton said. He was no science wiz, but he'd never heard of anything like this actually happening.

"In theory," Abigail said. "But not in real life."

"So this is a dream?" Colton said. "You know I hit my head earlier. This could all be my imagination."

"It could be," Abigail said. "But then I'd be imagining the same thing as you. And that's impossible."

"Not if you're in my imagination also," Colton said.

I'm not," Abigail said.

Colton poked her shoulder. "I could be imagining you saying that!"

She put her head in her hands and shook it. "Okay, let's just pretend that we're both not imagining this. And then, if it turns out that we are, it'll be really funny later. Ha ha. But for now, let's pretend."

Colton thought about this. It actually made good sense. He could pretend that he really was traveling in a spaceship at light speed. It was like a video game, not that he ever got to play video games since they couldn't afford a gaming console at home. But he'd seen his friends play plenty.

He felt his shoulders relax. This was much less stressful. Because otherwise, the entire situation was too impossible.

"What do we do now?" Colton asked.

Abigail pointed to a screen on the control panel. "This looks like a map of the galaxy. See how you can tell this is the Milky Way?"

"Sure." He nodded though he had no clue how she could tell that. But whatever. Maybe that wasn't important.

She might've known he was faking, but she still went on. "So yeah, it looks like we're traveling along a path. From here." She pointed to one spot. "To here." She pointed to another. "So I'm thinking that if this spaceship is really on autopilot—"

"On what?" Colton said.

"Autopilot," Abigail said. "That means it can drive itself. So if it is on autopilot, then we just have to wait until we reach our destination."

Wait? Colton was horrible at waiting.

"How long do you think it'll take?" he asked.

"Not much longer," Abigail said. "Look how fast we're moving across the map."

He watched a little dot of light on the galaxy map, zipping across the screen. And sure enough, after another couple minutes, the lights outside started slowing from long streaks into shorter streaks and then into pinpoint stars, like when he looked up into the night sky back in New Mexico. Except this was not New Mexico.

The spaceship finally slowed down to the point where it was barely drifting forward. Which was good, because right in front of them was a planet—a planet that was definitely not Earth.

CHAPTER 4

"Is that a—?" Colton started.

"A planet," Abigail said. "Sure looks like it."

"And I'm not imagining this either?" Colton said. At this point, if he was imagining everything, then he should start getting better grades on his creative writing assignments, because this was about as creative as it got. A story about this should get him an A plus.

"I don't think so," Abigail said. "You see how we're kind of spiraling into the planet, rather than going straight in? That's how the astronauts do it. It's supposed to be safer that way."

"Safer is good," Colton said.

The spaceship continued forward, spiraling down toward the planet. It kept a constant speed, which helped Colton keep his lunch in his stomach rather than all over the control board. All this light speed travel and liftoff stuff made him want to throw up. He'd managed to keep it together so far, but much more, and he couldn't make any promises.

The sky was dark, but as they got closer, it lightened, and pretty soon clouds appeared, just like on Earth.

Wait, had he really thought that? Just like on Earth? That was ridiculous. They should still be on Earth. Except they weren't. They were approaching some alien planet on the other side of the galaxy.

They passed through the clouds, and then the ship lowered straight down, keeping a steady pace. The closer they got, the more Colton could see. There were mountains and deserts. But there was no water. And no grass. No trees. No animals. Nothing living. It looked like the entire planet had died, like pictures he'd seen of Mars.

The spaceship finally landed on the ground. The second it did, the door that Colton had tried so hard to open earlier in the junkyard popped open all on its own, lifting up rather than out. So it hadn't been him. It was the whole autopilot thing. It had kept them locked in, which in hindsight was a good thing. Otherwise the door could have opened while they were traveling at light speed. That could have ripped the ship in half. Ripped his body in half. He'd be dead!

Colton unhooked his safety belt and jumped up from him seat. He immediately headed for the door.

"Wait!" Abigail said, grabbing his arm.

"Why?" he asked.

"Because you don't know what's out there," she said. "There could be man-eating aliens that are ready to have you for dinner."

Nothing had looked alive. Colton hoped she was being overly-cautious. Also, it was cool that he was about to explore somewhere besides Roswell, New Mexico.

"I'll take my chances," he said, and stepped out the door.

They had landed in the middle of the desert. Around them was nothing but sand.

"Is it safe?" Abigail called.

No man-eating aliens had gotten to him yet.

"It's safe," he said.

"Can you breathe?" she asked.

He took a deep breath. "Of course I can breathe. Why would I not be able to breathe?"

"Because," she said, stepping out next to him, "you don't know what kind of air the aliens who live here might breathe."

"They would breathe different air than us?" Colton said.

"Maybe," Abigail said. "You just don't know."

They took a few steps away from the spaceship so they could get a better view. In every direction, aside from them and their ship, was sand. Colton grabbed a handful and let it slip through his fingers. This was no different than back where they lived, in New Mexico. If this whole planet turned out to be as boring as back home, Colton was going to complain. Not that he knew who he'd complain to.

Far off in the distance, there was a single mountain. The sun—okay wait, there were two suns. Two suns! How was that even possible? Anyway—the suns shone light everywhere, and where it hit on top of the mountain, for a second it looked like it reflected off something.

"Do you see that?" Colton asked, pointing far off toward the mountain.

Abigail squinted. "Like a mirror or glass or something?" she said.

"Yeah," Colton said. "I think we should check it out."

They set out walking. The spaceship door stayed open, but Colton didn't think there was anyone around to mess with it. Also, when they were ready to return to Earth, they'd need to be able to get in. His feet sank in the sand, but he kept trudging, putting his head down to keep sand from blowing in his eyes. Pretty soon they got to the bottom of the mountain.

There, set into mountainside, was a stairway, made out of rocks that led up, all the way to the top. At the top, there was some kind of building.

Wait, not just a normal building. It looked like one of those ancient temples he'd seen in textbooks of ancient Greece and stuff like that, with big columns and lots of stone.

"We have to climb it," Abigail said.

"I know," Colton said. He was ready.

CHAPTER 5

It took way longer to reach the top of the mountain that Colton could have imagined. And the worst thing was that he was totally out of breath. Maybe the air was different here, because at home he played football and baseball and ran on the weekends. This should have been a piece of cake. When they finally made it to the top, he was gasping for air. Abigail was, too, which at least made him feel like less of a loser.

In front of them was a huge round stone building, with columns that stretched at least five stories high. There were all sorts of engravings on the stones, but they didn't look familiar. Instead it looked like a bunch of ancient symbols from an alphabet he'd never seen before.

"I think it's a temple," Colton whispered.

"Why are you whispering?" Abigail said.

"I don't know." There was just something about the place that made him feel the same way he felt inside a library, like if he talked loudly, the librarian would yell at him. And at this point he did not want to get in trouble. This was actually super cool.

"We should go inside," Abigail said, and she started forward.

Colton was right by her side, and even though he didn't know her at all, it was nice having someone else along, especially someone that wasn't making fun of the entire situation. His other friends would have been cracking jokes and pretending this was all a big hoax. But Colton wanted this to be real. And he was pretty sure that it was.

They climbed the steps of the giant temple—as if they hadn't climbed enough steps already—and went in. Inside was as big as a baseball field with no furniture, no chairs, or anything else that looked like it was from their world. Every wall was covered in the same symbols as outside along with all sorts of pictures. In the center of the room was a stone pedestal that had to be as wide as a sofa, and hovering above the pedestal was what Colton could only describe as a ball of energy.

It was red and black and crackled like small streaks of lightning ran through it. When Colton looked at it, it was like he could not stop himself from moving toward it. Abigail must've felt the same way, because she stayed right next to him, the whole way to the ball of energy.

No, not ball of energy.

Oracle.

That's what it was called. But how did he know that?

The name was there, in his mind. This was the Oracle. And they were on a planet named Xaxis.

"Are you getting the same thing that I am?" Colton asked, tapping the side of his head. He wasn't sure how else to phrase it. It wasn't talking to him. It was more like the names had been implanted in his head. Or like he'd always known them but hadn't known that he'd known them.

"Oracle of Xaxis," Abigail said.

"Right," Colton said. "But how . . . ?"

"I don't know," Abigail said.

They stopped when they were only a few yards away.

Closer, it seemed to say, even though it wasn't talking. Colton was sure of it. But still, they both stepped closer, until they were only a few feet away.

Closer, the Oracle seemed to say again.

They took one more step. That was as close as Colton planned to get.

"How's this?" he said, aloud.

"Perfect," the Oracle said, aloud this time. Colton looked to Abigail to make sure she'd heard it, too, and from her wide eyes, he knew she did.

"Why are we here?" Colton asked.

"Why are you where?" the Oracle said.

Colton motioned around the place, trying to show what he wanted to say. But it was no use.

"Xaxis," he said, knowing how to pronounce it since it had been planted in his head. It sounded like *Zak-sis*. Colton had no idea why people couldn't spell things the way they sounded. Also the letter X had never made much sense to Colton.

"The Oracle says that is just a simple Earth spelling," the Oracle said, as if it could read his mind.

Wait! Could it read his mind?

"The Oracle says yes," the Oracle said.

Colton put his head in his hand. Seriously? An alien . . . thing . . . could read his mind? That was so weird.

"Can we just answer the original question," Colton said. "Why are we here?"

"The Oracle says that you are here because the Xaxians brought you here," the Oracle said.

"Okay," Colton said. "Why did these Xaxians bring us here?"

"The Oracle says that you are already learning to ask the question you really want the answer to," the Oracle said.

This thing. It was not like Colton needed a lecture from some alien space temple thing.

"Anyway . . . ," he said.

"The Oracle says that—"

Colton put up his hand. "Can we stop with the whole 'The Oracle says' stuff?"

"The Oracle wonders how you will know who is speaking," the Oracle said.

"We'll know," Abigail said. "Trust us."

The Oracle flickered and flashed its lights like it was considering this. Then it said, "The Oracle agrees."

"So why are we here?" Colton said.

"The Or—You are here because your DNA has been matched. Your services are required to keep an alien race from taking over the entire galaxy," the Oracle said.

Colton looked to Abigail. DNA? Aliens? She looked as confused by all this as he was.

"You're saying that we need to save the galaxy?" Abigail said.

"That is what the Oracle is saying," the Oracle said. "You two, among all other creatures in the galaxy, have been selected for this very important task. You should feel highly honored."

Colton took a step back. "What if I don't want to save the galaxy? Why does the galaxy even need saved in the first place?"

"That is what the Oracle is about to tell you."

"Okay," Colton said, and waited.

The Oracle said nothing.

"Are you going to tell us?" Abigail asked.

"The Oracle was waiting for you to ask," the Oracle said. "You have been selected for a treasure hunt of most heroic proportions."

"A treasure hunt?" Colton said. "For real?" That was taking this whole thing a little too far. He didn't like treasure hunts. He didn't even like looking for a clean pair of socks. What Colton liked was sports and hanging out with his friends.

"A heroic treasure hunt," the Oracle said. "You have been tasked with seeking the Malevolent and Pure Tablet of Most Epic and Scintillating Power." It said this last bit with a huge flourish, and its voice echoed throughout the chamber.

"The what?" Abigail said, and it looked like she was trying to count the words on her fingers.

"The Malevolent and Pure Tablet of Most Epic and Scintillating Power," the Oracle said again.

"A tablet?" Colton said. "You want us to find some kind of tablet?"

"That does simplify it, though still remains correct," the Oracle said, and Colton would have sworn it sounded disappointed.

"Okay, how do we find it?" Colton asked. They could find this tablet and get back to Earth before dinner. Not that space travel wasn't kind of cool and all, but Colton had other things to do. Or at least he should have other things to do. Forget that he was bored to tears an hour ago.

"The Malevolent and Pure Tablet of Most Epic and Scintillating Power has been—" the Oracle started.

"Can we just call it the Tablet?" Colton said.

"So simple, but if that is all your petty Earthling brains can handle, then the Oracle agrees," the Oracle said.

Colton felt like he should have been offended, but was just happy that the Oracle had agreed.

"The Tablet has been separated into six pieces. Each piece is on a different planet. You will need to travel to each of these planets, find the Malevolent and—the Tablet piece, and bring it back here."

"Six planets!" Colton said. That was not going to happen. "How on Earth are we supposed to do that?"

"We're not on Earth," Abigail said, elbowing him to maybe get him to shut up.

"Okay, fine," Colton said. "How do we do that? Why do we do that? Can we get a bit more information?"

The Oracle crackled with light again. "All the information you require is encoded on the walls of this temple."

Colton looked at the weird symbols and pictures. "We can't read that." He turned to Abigail. "Can we?" Maybe she could read the weird alien writing.

Abigail shook her head.

"Xaxians must have thought Earthlings would be more intelligent," the Oracle said, and it seemed bothered that it had to explain. "One hundred thousand years ago, the Xaxians created the Tablet. It held all the power of the universe. They used it for only good, but then other alien races tried to steal the Tablet. The Xaxians realized that it would always be a target and that the galaxy would never be safe so long as the Tablet existed. But they couldn't bring themselves to destroy it. They'd worked too hard on it. So instead they broke it into six pieces and hid the pieces around the galaxy."

"That's pretty cool," Abigail said. "It really is like a treasure hunt."

Colton didn't want to admit it out loud, but she was right. Aliens and tablets of power were kind of awesome. But that still didn't explain what they were doing here.

"But why does it have to be found?" Colton asked. "Why can't it just stay hidden?"

"For thousands of years, the Tablet only existed as a legend," the Oracle said. "It was forgotten. But recent events have changed that."

"What recent events?" Abigail asked.

"Ickians," the Oracle said.

"Ickians?" Colton said. It almost sounded like the Oracle had something caught in its throat.

"Ickians," the Oracle said. "They are the despicable alien race that destroyed the entire race of Xaxians."

"That's why no one lives on this planet?" Abigail said. "Because another alien race destroyed them?"

"Correct," the Oracle said. "The Ickians came here to get information on the location of the Tablet, and when they did, the Ickians started the apocalypse. Every living thing on the planet died."

Wow. That was actually pretty horrible. Colton could see why aliens like the Ickians shouldn't have something with a lot of power, like the Tablet.

"Wait a minute," Abigail said. "If everyone who lived on this planet was killed, how did the spaceship that we flew in get to Earth in the first place?"

Lightning sizzled inside the Oracle. "The Xaxians were only able to send out a handful of rescue ships, one to your planet. They were programmed with the location of this planet and were designed to activate when the correct DNA triggered them. In the case of Earth, it was your DNA."

"You're saying that of all the people on Earth, you guys thought we were the ones to save the world?" Colton said.

"Not the world," the Oracle said. "The entire galaxy. Maybe the universe. You cannot let the Ickians get the pieces of the Tablet, because if they do, they will conquer one planet after the next, including your own home planet, Earth."

"They're going to destroy Earth?" Colton said.

"Not if we stop them," Abigail said.

She was right. As crazy as this entire thing was, that did seem like what they had to do.

"Okay," Colton said. "Let's just pretend that we're going to go on your treasure hunt. What are we supposed to do?"

"You've each been given a ring," the Oracle said.

Colton looked at his hand. The Oracle was right! There was a ring on his finger with a big blue alien head on it, like some cheesy cheap knickknack that tourists flocked to Roswell to buy.

"The ring is synchronized with this temple," the Oracle said. "When it lights up, you are to get in your spaceship and travel here to Xaxis. At that point, the location for the next piece of the Tablet will be revealed. You will then retrieve the Tablet piece and bring it back here to be collected. When all six pieces have been collected, the Tablet can be destroyed."

Colton shook his head. "That seems like a big waste of time. Why don't you just give us all the locations right now? We'll zip around from one planet to the next and get them all." To him, it sounded like the perfect plan.

"Silly, impatient Earthlings," the Oracle said, making it sound like it was the most ridiculous suggestion in the universe. "All the locations cannot be given at once.

That would allow alien races like the Ickians to easily get the Tablet. It is a risk that cannot be taken."

Okay, fine. So this Oracle thing had a good point.

Something caught Colton's eye. He looked down. The blue alien head on his ring was glowing.

"And now it's time," the Oracle said. "The location of the first Tablet piece will be revealed."

CHAPTER 6

The Oracle changed color, from red and black to a bright blue, just like the alien head on the ring. But it didn't rattle off the location of the first Tablet piece, like Colton figured it would. Instead it began to spin, around and around, getting faster every second. Pretty soon it looked like nothing but a huge blue blur.

Just when Colton was about to look away, because if he had to be honest, it was kind of making him want to throw up, it stopped spinning. Bright white light shot out of it, in a single laser beam, and lit up a spot on the wall.

"Over there!" Abigail yelled, and she grabbed his arm and dragged him toward the spot on the wall that was lit up.

Of the jumble of symbols and pictures on the wall, a single circle was illuminated.

Abigail pointed to it. "That's it! The locations of all the pieces are on the walls on this temple. But there's no way to know where without the Oracle pointing to it."

Colton leaned close, trying to make sense of the symbols. "Can you read it?"

She rubbed her eyes and put her face closer. "My mom brings stuff like this home all the time."

"Alien writings?" Colton said. "What? Is she an alien?"

Abigail laughed. "No, she's a linguist. She teaches at the university. But in her spare time, she decodes all sorts of ancient relics, you know, like archaeology type stuff. She's always saying that none of the little pictures are random. And that so many of the alphabets are actually designed the way they are on purpose. Like there's a reason for it. This has to be the same thing. You see this part here?" She pointed to one area in the upper right. "I bet that's a star pattern that's supposed to tell us where to actually fly to in space. And this part here, it look like a map of a planet. And maybe a big Nebula. And see this? This is like a city. And—"

As she was talking, the circle of light slowly started to fade.

"I trust you," Colton said. "Just get what you can before it disappears."

Abigail nodded and moved her head up and down, studying all the different parts of the wall writings. Colton did the same, focusing on the part she'd said looked like a map. He was pretty good with maps. He tried to remember as many of the symbols as he could. But every second the light shining from the Oracle got dimmer and dimmer, until finally it went out altogether.

Colton stepped back and blinked. He tried to focus on the wall again, in the same spot, except nothing looked the same. It was like other symbols had been carved on top of the ones they were looking at and there was no way to tell them apart.

"It's like an illusion," Colton said. "And some of the symbols vanish when the light shines on them."

"It's okay," Abigail said. "I think I got it. I'm pretty good at remembering things."

Colton hoped so because all he'd managed to remember was maybe five symbols at the most.

He turned back to the Oracle. It shifted back to a red and black ball of energy, and it was silent. They'd gotten all the information that they were going to out of it.

"Ready?" he asked.

Abigail let out another laugh. "No. But I don't think that matters."

They left the temple, and a moment of pure joy filled Colton. They didn't have to go up any more stairs. Only down. That was so much better and took a lot less time. That was the best part of this whole adventure so far.

Fine. The alien temple place was pretty cool, too. And the treasure hunt thing. It was like a game. That was how he was going to think of it. A game that he got to play while his friends were off at summer camp. They were probably having a miserable time, stepping in bear poop and scrubbing the camp counselors' toilets. He was going to save the galaxy!

The spaceship was exactly where they'd left it, with the door still open. Abigail climbed in first and Colton followed. The door immediately closed.

She pressed a few buttons on the control panel.

"Watch what you press," Colton said.

"I know what I'm doing," Abigail said.

41

He had no clue how that could be possible. But whatever.

The map screen lit up, and she started using her finger to move the picture on it around. "What we have to do is find the stars on this map that look like the ones from the temple . . . Oh, there they are." She zoomed in on a specific area and tapped her finger right in the middle. It lit up with a red dot. "This is where we need to go."

That was awesome. But it also made Colton feel kind of worthless. If she could use the controls, so could he. He thought back and tried to remember which buttons had been lit up when they'd been flying. He was almost sure of at least two of them.

"Then here we go," Colton said. "Liftoff!" He pressed one of the buttons, the biggest one since that made the most sense.

The spaceship launched up into the air, way faster than the last time. But it didn't matter. They were on their way. They were going to save the galaxy.

CHAPTER 7

"What did you do?" Abigail shouted. She kept trying to reach for the control panel, but the spaceship was moving so fast that she and Colton were slammed back into their seats like bugs on a windshield.

"I started the spaceship," Colton said. "We're on our way!"

Abigail finally managed to reach the controls and pressed something. The ship immediately slowed down. By now they were way above the planet. Or at least he assumed they were. Since there was only one window—

the front one—it wasn't like he could turn around and look.

"Next time, let me do it," Abigail said.

"No way," Colton said. "I can fly the spaceship, too."

"Really?" she said. "Because it seemed more like you were trying to kill us. Just let me do it."

Colton was not about to admit it, but she was right. He had no clue what the controls did. She pressed a few more buttons—he watched and tried to remember which ones—and the ship turned and did that hovering thing. They were about to jump to light speed. He knew it. His stomach tensed in anticipation. But he also hated this whole feeling useless thing. He was not useless!

"Okay, wait," he said. "How about all these other controls? What can I do? I need some kind of job. You shouldn't be the only one who gets to push buttons."

Abigail rolled her eyes. "Fine. How about you can be in charge of avoiding space debris and general security?"

"Really?" Colton said. He heard the excitement in his voice and tried to tone it down. "I mean, that sounds okay, I guess. What should I do?"

She reached over and flipped five different switches. Immediately five different screens lit up, each showing outer space. And there, on one of them, was the planet they'd just come from, Xaxis.

"These are cameras," Colton said. It was just like the backup camera in his dad's truck.

"Yep," she said. "You can tell me when we need to change course to avoid space junk, and keep a watch for anything unusual."

"Like what?" Colton said. Everything so far was unusual as far as he was concerned.

"I don't know," Abigail said. "But you'll know it when you see it. So now that we have that settled, are we ready to go?"

"We're ready," Colton said. He clicked his safety belt. He'd have to remember to do that first thing when he got in next time.

Next time. What a weird thought. Anyway . . .

"Light speed engage!" Abigail said, and even though it sounded completely dorky, it was also kind of awesome.

She pressed a button, and the spaceship jumped forward. The stars turned into long streaks of light again. Colton's stomach lurched, but the urge to throw up was way less than last time. On the map screen, he watched as the red blip that was their ship traveled across the galaxy to the location Abigail had programmed in.

Then, for the rest of the time, they sat there, making the most awkward small talk in the entire universe. But seriously, what did he have in common with this girl? Nothing, that's what. He liked sports and hanging out with friends, and she probably didn't ever leave her house. Except . . .

"What were you doing in the junkyard anyway?" Colton asked.

"Nothing," Abigail said.

"Really?" he said. "You risked having that monster dog tear your arm off for nothing?"

"Ogre," she said.

"What?"

"His name is Ogre," Abigail said. "The dog. And he's not that scary."

"Is that why you were hiding from him behind a car?" Colton said, but he shook his head. "Never mind. Why were you there? For real."

She fiddled with some of the controls. "It's just this hobby I have."

"Playing in junkyards?" Colton said.

"Looking for parts," Abigail said. "I create things out of old stuff."

"Like art?"

"Sometimes," Abigail said. "But also inventions, and I fix things and stuff like that. That junkyard is crazy. Have you seen some of the stuff they have?" She shoved her hand in her pocket and pulled out what looked like a big glob of wires and a metal gear. "Like check this out. I've been looking for one of these things forever. And I finally found it."

"That's great," Colton said, though he didn't have a clue what it was. He decided not to ask, since then she'd think he was even dumber than she already did.

Something beeped, and before Colton could look at the map screen, they dropped out of light speed travel. There in front of them was another planet, but this one was green and blue and looked a lot like Earth.

A voice came on over a speaker in the spaceship, but it wasn't the same voice they'd heard when they first got in. This was almost like it was coming through some kind of intercom.

"Greetings, alien spaceship, and welcome to the planet Micron," the voice said.

Colton looked at Abigail but didn't say a word. She bit her lip and looked like she would have turned the spaceship back and flown the other way if she could. Aliens! They were going to have to deal with real live aliens.

"Please state the name of your vehicle and your destination," the voice said.

"What's the name of our ship?" Colton whispered.

"Um . . . ," Abigail said.

Wait, was she nervous? She was! But he wasn't. This was perfect. She may be all great at flying the ship and stuff, but this was Colton's specialty. He loved talking to people. Talking was what he did best.

He pressed the button next to the speaker on the control panel.

"Greetings, Planet Micron," Colton said in his most official sounding voice. "This is the spaceship . . . " His mind spun as he tried to think something up. "This is the Spaceship Ogre requesting permission to land. We're heading to the Nebula City."

He hoped he got the name right. Abigail had told him during the awkward small talk part of their trip.

"You mean the Nebula District?" the voice said.

"Affirmative," Colton said. "Spaceship Ogre headed to the Nebula District."

"Confirmed," the voice said. "What is your purpose for visiting?"

Purpose? They couldn't state their real purpose.

"We're tourists," Colton said. "We've come for . . . "
He knew nothing about this planet. Why did anyone come to Planet Micron?

"The Micron Meltaways?" the voice said, helpfully.

"Affirmative again," Colton said. "We've come for the Micron Meltaways."

Whatever they were.

"Thank you, Spaceship Ogre," the voice said. "You may proceed. Enjoy your time on Planet Micron."

Abigail blew out a deep breath that she must have been holding this entire time, and then she changed the controls and they started their descent.

"That was so cool!" Colton said. "But how can we understand them? You think they speak Earthling all the way out here?"

"You mean English?" Abigail said.

"Right, English."

"I think it's some kind of universal translator," she said. "But whatever it is, it sure will make things easier."

The ship circled around, just like it had done before, getting closer and closer to the planet. Colton watched the whole thing both out the front window and on the viewing screens in front of him. Once they were really close, a city came into view.

"That's the Nebula District," Abigail said, pointing.

49

It looked like there was a big parking lot for space-ships, and Colton had to give her credit, because she steered the ship right into a spot.

"Nice job," he said. "You only almost hit three oth-er spaceships."

"Almost doesn't count," Abigail said, pressing the button to turn off their ship—Ogre. It was a great name for a spaceship.

Immediately the door popped open.

Outside were aliens. Bunches and bunches of aliens. They walked around everywhere. Well, some of them were walking around. Some jumped because they only had one leg. A couple rolled, like giant roly-polies. Some alien with eight eyes that looked a lot like a spi-der glanced over and them, shrugged, and then looked away. Colton hated spiders.

But still, that was good. At least they'd blend in.

"We should shut the door," Abigail said.

None of the other spaceships in the parking lot had their doors hanging open, so it seemed like a good idea. But no amount of tugging on the door lowered it. That's when Colton noticed the flat panel on the side of the spaceship. Abigail must've noticed it, too, be-cause she placed her hand on it, palm down. The door immediately closed.

"Must be coded to our DNA," Abigail said, like that was all normal and stuff.

"Yeah, must be," he said, trying to act unimpressed.

Now to try this universal translator stuff.

Colton walked over to three aliens that were standing together. Okay, not standing. They floated in the air, hovering about half a foot off the ground with huge wings extended behind them.

"Hey, what's up?" he said, waving.

The three aliens leapt backward. "Do you challenge us?" the biggest one said. They were all three covered in green feathers, but his feathers seemed the brightest.

"No, of course not," Colton said. "I'm just saying hi." He waved again.

This apparently didn't sit well, because all three opened their mouths, exposing spiky teeth that Colton would have sworn were not there two seconds before.

"We accept your challenge," the alien said. "Prepare to die."

CHAPTER 8

olton put up both hands. "No, wait a second. I was just waving." He was about to show them, but then figured it might not be a good idea.

"On our world, that is an invitation for a death match," the alien said.

Colton laughed and smiled and shook his head. "Oh, no, that's not what I meant at all! On our world, that's how we say hello."

The three aliens seemed to consider this for a second, and it must've gone well, because they tucked their fang teeth back into their mouths and lowered their wings, drifting to the ground.

"In that case, hello," the alien said.

Whew. That had been close. Colton made a note to be a little more careful. The last thing he needed was getting them killed before they'd even left the parking lot.

"Hi," Colton said, making sure not to wave. "We were wondering if you could point us to the city. We're in Nebula District, right?"

"Oh, sure," the alien said. "The main sector of Nebula District is just over that way." He used a wing to point the direction.

"Thanks!" Colton said. "Well, maybe we'll see you around!"

"Yes, see you around," the alien said, and Colton would have sworn he waved with his wing!

Was that a challenge? Seriously? Colton pretended that he didn't see.

He waited until they were well away from the aliens before speaking. "Wow, that was close."

"Try not to get us killed next time, okay?" Abigail said.

"How was I supposed to know I couldn't wave?" Colton said. "That's got to be the dumbest thing I've ever heard in my life. A death match? And there have to be fifty different kinds of aliens around here. What if they all have different customs?"

"We can help you with alien customs if you'd like," someone said.

They'd just reached the inside of the city and were in some kind of big outdoor shopping area. Aliens were selling food and clothes and postcards with pictures of the planet on them. Maybe he should get one and mail it to his friends at summer camp. See what they thought of that.

He looked around to see who'd spoken. Behind him and Abigail stood two super skinny aliens with pasty white skin and faces that looked like they'd been pinched with a clothespin. One was seriously tall, like he'd have hit his pinchy head on every door back on Earth, and the other was short enough to pass for a first grader.

"Oh, hi," Colton said, making sure not to wave, even though these aliens were way different that the green feathered ones. "You know about alien customs?"

"Yes," the shorter of the aliens said. "We can tell you anything you need to know."

"Anything!" the taller alien said.

"Great!" Colton said. "Who can I wave to? And what else can I not do? Like can I not smile at certain aliens? Or what about a high five? And blinking. Am I allowed to blink?"

He noticed that neither of these two aliens were blinking, but then it didn't look like they had eyelids, so that made sense.

"So many questions," the taller alien said. "But how rude of me. I never introduced myself. My name is Farp and this is my friend Vomix."

"Farp and Vomix?" Colton said, trying to keep from laughing.

"Farp and Vomix," Farp said. "At your service. We can tell you anything you need to know."

Next to Colton, Abigail burst out laughing. Colton tried everything he could to not join in.

"Micron Meltaways for sale!" one of the vendors nearby shouted across the crowd. "Best in the galaxy. Melt in your mouth. Get your Micron Meltaways!"

That's what the person in charge of the planet had told them tourists came for. Micron Meltaways. Colton made a note to check it out because his stomach was kind of grumbling.

"Are you guys from this planet?" Colton said. "Like are you Micronians?" He figured that's what the aliens of Micron would be called.

"Not us," Vomix said. "We're Ickians."

Ickians! No way! These were the aliens that were trying to get the pieces of the Tablet. The ones who had killed off the entire Xaxian race. It could not be a coincidence that they were here, right now, talking to Colton and Abigail.

Colton saw Abigail's eyes widen. He mentally tried to tell her not to say a word about it.

"Never heard of Ickians," Colton said. "Anyway, we're off to get a Micron Meltaway, but maybe we'll catch you later."

Colton grabbed Abigail's arm and dragged her away from the Ickians, toward the alien selling the food.

"Those were Ickians!" Abigail said. "They're the ones—"

"I know," Colton said. "Just act normal. But keep your eyes on them."

She swiveled her head back to look at the Ickians.

"No," Colton said. "Don't let them know we're watching them."

He walked up to the alien with the basket of Micron Meltaways. They were pink and green and yellow and looked like cubes of creamy milk. Colton could almost imagine it melting in his mouth. The alien was a kind of sick-looking mixture of green and yellow and had four arms. Maybe he was a Micronian.

"How many?" the alien said.

That's when the horrible realization hit Colton. They didn't have any money.

"We don't have any cash," Abigail said, eyeing the candies longingly.

The alien's face hardened. "Well, no cash, no—"

"Yeah," Colton said before the alien could finish. "Those Ickians stole it from us." He did his best to look sad and angry, all the while keeping his fingers crossed.

Maybe the alien took pity on them, because he said, "Ickians! That riffraff shouldn't even be allowed to land here. Can't trust 'em." And he handed them each a Micron Meltaway.

Colton immediately dropped it onto his tongue. It was like sugar and honey and ice cream all mixed in on, like a tiny piece of paradise. And it really did melt in his mouth. Colton could've probably eaten twenty more, but he didn't push his luck.

"Any idea where we can get a map?" Abigail said once her meltaway was gone.

The alien pointed with one of his hands toward a row of shops. "Pretty sure the shop in the middle has some. But don't think the owner will give you a freebee even if the Ickians took your money. She's old and bitter and hates tourists. You're going to need some cash."

CHAPTER 9

C ash! Why did everything always come down to cash? Colton didn't have any now, but that wasn't any different than normal. Unlike all his friends, his family never had spare money.

"Maybe we can just look at the map," Abigail said. "Maybe we won't have to buy it."

They started to walk over to the shop, but something ran up to them and pounced on Colton. Since he wasn't expecting it, it almost knocked him over. He looked down, and there was a tiny little dog, wagging its tail.

Wait! That wasn't a tail! Or was it? It almost looked like a scorpion's tail, with a giant spike on the end. It whapped back and forth, barely missing his arm.

"What in the world are you?" Colton said to the dog. "I mean in the galaxy! What in the galaxy!?"

Its ears swiveled around and the tail wagged more. Nope, wrong again. Those weren't ears. They were antennae. And its paws were at least four times too big for its body.

"It's an alien dog," Colton said.

"I think it likes us," Abigail said, because once they started walking again, the thing stuck right next to them. Maybe it was because they were the only ones who looked normal on this entire planet. Of course, to all the aliens on the planet, they didn't look normal at all, but whatever.

The door to the shop slid open, but inside wasn't some cheap little tourist trap filled with postcards like Colton had expected on a tourist planet. Instead, it looked like a curiosity shop, with so many random knickknacks, it made Colton's head spin.

"Look at this place," Abigail said, running to the counter.

"Stop!" the grumpy alien woman behind the counter said. She looked a lot like the Micron Meltaway guy, with four arms, but she had a lot more wrinkles covering her green and yellow skin. "No Zeros allowed inside!"

Colton looked from himself to Abigail.

"What's a zero?" Colton asked.

The alien woman pointed to the dog thing. "That's a zero. Leave it outside. If it poops on my floor, you two are cleaning it up."

The dog was so small, Colton couldn't imagine it making much of a mess, but he didn't want to find out. He went back out and pointed right next to the door. "Stay here," he said.

The dog did exactly what he said!

"Good, Zero," Colton said, and went back inside. Maybe Zeros were like Earth dogs except way smarter.

By the time he got back inside, Abigail already had five things out on the counter that she was looking at, picking each one up and studying it before moving on to the next.

"Do they have a map?" Colton asked. There was no reason to waste time looking at a bunch of stuff they didn't need. What they did need was to look at the map and figure out where they had to go to find the artifact.

"Map?" the alien woman said. "Why do you want a map? Nobody can get lost in Nebula District."

This seemed to get Abigail's attention back on their mission.

"We need a really old map," Abigail said. "Like something that might show how things looked . . . oh, I don't know . . . thousands of years ago, before all the shops and tourists and stuff like that?"

The alien woman's eyes narrowed, making her wrinkles look even bigger than they already did. "Why do little tourist kids like you two want something like that?"

Colton looked to Abigail.

"We're linguists," Abigail said. "We're doing research on alien languages around the galaxy. So an old map will really help us discover how the Micronian language was developed."

Ten points for Abigail. That was a perfect answer.

The alien woman seemed completely unimpressed. "Yeah, whatever floats your boat. I have some old maps. Right over there."

She pointed with one of her four hands to a shelf where at least twenty pieces of wood were stacked. Each was like an inch thick, and all were covered with dust, like no one had ever looked at them, including the alien woman. If they were maps, it couldn't hurt to take a peek at a few.

Colton hurried over and lifted the first one. "Which is the oldest?"

But the woman snatched it out of his hands before he could see a single landmark.

"You have to pay first," she said, setting the map back down.

"Oh, about that," Colton said, trying to sweet talk her, even though she was completely old and bitter like the Meltaway guy had said. But Colton could talk his way into anything. This should be no problem. "See, there were these Ickians, and they took our—"

The alien held up one of her hands. "Boo hoo. Your sad little sob story won't work on me. Cash or no map."

But they really needed the map. Like really really needed the map. This was about saving the galaxy.

Abigail looked like she was holding back on saying something, but then finally couldn't stand it anymore. "How about a trade?" she said. She reached into her pocket and pulled out the wire gear thing that she'd showed him earlier. This was the part that she'd been looking for forever. The one she'd found in the junk-yard. She couldn't give it away.

The alien woman took it with one of her hands and flipped it around to get a better look at it. She didn't ask what it was. Maybe she already knew, or maybe she didn't care.

"Where'd a little punk like you get this?" the alien said. "Did ya steal it? Because I don't take stolen goods. I'll call the guards on you."

Abigail looked like she wanted to grab it back, but she kept her hands at her sides. "I didn't steal it. I got it on Earth," she said. "That's the planet we're from."

There wasn't much point in lying. It's not like whatever this thing happened to be was in such high demand that aliens were going to invade Earth to get more.

"Earth, huh," the woman said. "Never heard of it. Sounds like a bowel sickness."

How rude was that? This alien woman didn't know anything about polite conversation.

She looked at it some more. "This is pretty unique though."

"Unique enough for a trade?" Colton said hopefully.

She seemed to consider this, then finally said, "One map. You get one map."

Abigail took one final look at the gear thing before the alien woman slipped it into a pocket.

Colton started flipping through the maps on the shelf. One map. That was all they needed. But it had to be the right one. The maps were actually wooden blocks that had carvings, showing rivers and mountains and stuff from all around the planet. But they didn't need to go just anywhere on the planet. They'd come here to Nebula District because that's what the directions in the temple had said.

Next to him, Abigail was also going through the maps, saying, "Not this one. Not this one. Nope. No again." And as the stacks got shorter, Colton started worrying that they wouldn't find anything useful.

"Nope," Abigail said, and set a map down.

Colton immediately picked it up. He'd only seen it out of the corner of his eye, but something about it had gotten his attention.

He scoured it, trying to figure out what. And there it was. Three hills near the top of the map.

"This," he said, pointing at the hill formation. It wasn't that there were just three hills. It was the way they were placed, in a row. It looked exactly like pictures he'd seen of how the Egyptian pyramids were arranged back on Earth. And it also looked exactly like the symbols on the wall of the temple back on Xaxis.

Abigail leaned close to get a better look. "I think you're right," she said.

"Of course I'm right," Colton said. "Why do you make it sound like that's impossible?"

She shrugged. "I don't know. It's just that I didn't see it, I guess."

Colton couldn't keep the smug look off his face. He might not have a mom who was a linguist, but he could remember things like they pyramids that he'd seen pictures of before. He'd never have told his friends because they would have laughed, but when he was really little, and his friends would all go on vacation, he used to pretend to visit cool places all over the world. Egypt had been one of those places.

"Do you know where this place is?" Colton asked, showing the alien woman.

She looked like she couldn't be bothered with the question. She was too busy trying to pull the wires off the gear thing Abigail had given her.

"Nope, sorry," she said. "But if you ever come back, I'm always up for a trade. This is going to get me a fortune."

If the Ickians got the pieces of the Tablet, it wouldn't matter. They'd take over this world and any others they could. But so far, Colton and Abigail were doing pretty great. They were on their way to getting the first piece. Everything was going their way. That all changed the second they walked out the door. Three Micronian guards were outside waiting.

"You're being placed under arrest," one guard said, and he grabbed Colton's arm.

Colton glanced to Abigail, hoping they were thinking the same thing. Apparently they were. He yanked his arm from the guard's hand, and they took off running.

CHAPTER 10

C olton didn't look back. Abigail ran next to him, totally keeping pace on one side. On the other was Zero, the alien dog thing, following along. Its tiny legs scrambled but kept up. They ducked around a corner and then another one really fast, managing to lose the alien guards.

Zero's antennae swiveled around and reached way forward, like he was listening to some far-off conversation. Sure enough, the three Micronian guards came into view seconds later. They'd stopped and were looked around everywhere, talking into some kind of alien walkie-talkie things. Zero let out a low growl.

"Quiet, boy," Colton said, putting his hand on the dog's back. He hoped the scorpion tail didn't jab down and spike him.

"What do you think they want?" Abigail said while they hid behind some barrels.

"No idea," Colton said.

But then it became perfectly obvious. The two Ickians, Farp and Vomix came into view and hurried over to the guards. They started talking and pointing and making all sorts of gestures. Maybe the Ickians would mess up and use some gesture requesting a fight to the death, like Colton had almost done. Zero spotted them also and started growling.

"They want to get us arrested so they can get the Tablet piece," Abigail said.

As much as he might not have wanted it to be true, it totally was. Getting arrested and thrown into some alien jail was the last thing they needed.

"We need to get to the Tablet piece first," Colton said. He held the map in front of them so they could spend more time studying at it. So far, the three alien guards were not looking their way.

"There's not even a city on this map," Abigail said. "How are we supposed to know where anything is?"

"We look for things that might be the same," Colton said. "Like this river up here. And these other hills on either side. I bet we can still find those." Growing up, he'd spent more time exploring Roswell than hanging out at home. He'd gotten pretty good at directions.

"Good point," Abigail said, tracing her finger along the link of the river. "But the river . . . we don't have any clue which way to even go. And with those guards looking for us, we don't have all day."

"Leave that to me," Colton said.

They waited for the guards to leave, and then crept out from their hiding spot. Colton led the way, moving down the street, turning left then right then left again. They had to get away from anywhere the guards had been looking, just in case there was some kind of reward for turning them in. When he figured they were finally in safe territory, he walked up to the nearest food cart. It had vegetables, not Micron Meltaways like he'd hoped. Even though nothing on this cart looked like what they had back on Earth, there was no way to disguise broccoli no matter what planet you were on.

Two aliens ran the food cart, both Micronians based on their number of arms.

"Which way to the river?" Colton asked the aliens.

"North River or South River?" one of the Micronians said.

North or south? How was Colton supposed to know that? He thought about the map. Sure, they wanted to go toward the top of the map, but that didn't mean anything. They were on a planet halfway across the galaxy, not Earth. Anything was possible.

"Which one has more hills around it?" Colton asked.

"Hills?" the other alien said. "That's the South River you want." The alien pointed off in the distance. "You want to go that way. Maybe two miles. You can't miss it."

This was perfect! Now, at least, they knew which way to go. Colton was about to thank the aliens, when from behind him, he heard someone say, "Earthlings? I saw Earthlings."

He spun around. Abigail stood there with a panicked look on her face. The three alien guards were just finishing up talking to someone and turned their heads, spotting Colton and Abigail immediately.

"Thanks!" Colton said to the aliens, and he and Abigail took off running.

They wove through the streets and between buildings, and Colton did his best to keep track of which

71

way they were going. They could still hear a bunch of noises and shouts from behind them, so he was sure the guards were still after them.

"This way," Colton said, turning down an alley.

Thankfully, it was empty. They hurried forward, Zero at their feet. And when they came to the end, Colton zipped around the corner. This was where they would lose the guards. Except that's not what happened at all. When they turned the corner, there stood one of the guards, all four arms extended to block their path.

"Retreat!" Abigail shouted.

But when they turned back, there were the other two guards. They were trapped.

CHAPTER 11

"You are under arrest," one of the guards said.

"Arrest!" Abigail said. "What for? We didn't do anything."

"That's not what's been reported," the guard said, and before either of them could say another word, the guard slapped some kind of handcuffs on their wrists. The only thing is that the handcuffs must've been designed for the Micronians because there were locks for four arms instead of two.

Colton struggled against them, but that only made them get tighter.

"What's been reported?" Colton said, trying not to move his hands. If there was any chance of getting these things off, making them tighter wasn't going to help.

"A formal accusation will be made at the police station," one of the guards said. "Until then, we are not allowed, by law, to say a word."

That was just perfect. The guards hauled them through the city—which was totally embarrassing and almost certainly not giving anyone a good first impression of Earthlings—then down steps that led underground into some sort of concrete cell block. Aliens were locked up in cells all along the hallway. Colton would have sworn he saw the green feathered aliens from the parking lot. Maybe they'd gotten in one too many death matches. The guards dragged them to the end and opened one of the cells.

"There you go," the guard said.

Colton and Abigail didn't move.

"What do you mean, there we go?" Colton said. "We're not going in there."

"Sure you are," the guard said. "But the good news is that when you do go in there, like I know you're going to, I can take off your handcuffs."

Tempting, except not. The guard had used some kind of swipe card to unlock the door. They didn't have one of those cards. If they went into the cell, they'd be stuck.

But Abigail said, "Okay," and walked in the cell. The guard unlocked her handcuffs. She looked at Colton as if to say, 'Get your idiot bottom in here.'

So Colton went in.

The guard unlocked his handcuffs, too, and then shut the door, locking them in.

"Now can you tell us what we've been accused of?" Colton said.

"Sure," the alien said. "It was reported that you've come to Planet Micron to steal national treasures."

"National treasures!" Abigail said. "Who accused us?"

"Two fine Ickian ambassadors," the guard said.

The Ickians! Colton knew it. But they were trying to steal the Tablet piece also. Mentioning this wouldn't get them out of the cell, so Colton kept his mouth shut.

"How long do we have to stay here?" Colton asked. Maybe they'd be let out after an hour. Still, an hour was too long. The Ickians would get the Tablet before them.

"Five years," the guard said. "But don't worry. Prisoners receive a Micron Meltaway every Friday at lunch. Enjoy!"

With that, he walked away.

"Five years!" Colton said. "Is that guy kidding?"

Abigail was hardly listening, though. Instead she was at the door, fiddling with the lock. And then Colton remembered how she'd said she was good about building stuff and things like that.

"You think you can get us out?" he asked.

Abigail smiled. "I'm sure of it. This is a simple lock. I can't believe they actually use it. A baby could break out of this cell."

Colton didn't think she was right. The lock looked more complicated that a scientific calculator. But Abigail seemed to know what she was doing. She poked and prodded at it and pulled some kind of panel off and started messing with wires.

"Stop!" Colton said, because from around the corner a guard came into view.

They both backed up against the wall and waited until the guard had passed. Once he was out of sight, she went at it again, touching a bunch of wires together. Colton figured either the entire thing would blow up like some kind of bomb, or she'd get it unlocked.

Luckily, it was the latter.

The lock clicked and popped open.

"Nice!" Colton said, and put up his hand for a high five.

Abigail looked at his hand.

"You're supposed to slap it with you hand," Colton said. How could she not know that? Everyone knew what a high five was.

"I know," Abigail said. "But it's not like you've ever talked to me in school, and now you're being all nice to me? What's up with that?"

Colton kept his hand up. "Well, we are kind of a team now. Saving the galaxy together, side by side. Right?"

She narrowed her eyebrows as she seemed to think about this, and then finally returned the high five. Then they got the heck out of there, running down the hall the way they'd come. Colton thought he heard a shout or two from behind them, but he didn't stick around to find out.

At the top of the stairs, Zero appeared. Colton hadn't even seen the alien dog waiting. His scorpion tail started wagging the instant he saw them, and he let out another bark. Then he starting running and turning back, like he was trying to tell them which way to go. There was no time to waste.

Colton looked to Abigail who nodded her head.

"Let's go," she said, and they took off running, after the alien dog.

CHAPTER 12

Zero led them through the city, almost like he knew exactly where they wanted to go.

Wait. Was Zero a boy dog? A girl dog? Colton had no idea.

Anyway, the dog let out a bark every so often to get their attention, but kept running, and they following. Finally, Abigail stopped running.

"We need to take a break," she said, leaning against some sort of space speeder that looked a lot like a motorcycle. It wobbled at her weight, but stayed upright, and it floated above the ground rather than standing on wheels.

"We have to keep going," Colton said. The Ickians could not get there first. They already had too big of a head start.

"Two minutes," Abigail said, catching her breath.

If only they had money. It looked like the speeders were for rent, because they were locked up and had slots nearby that maybe Micronians put money in to borrow them.

Borrow them. Wait! That was all they needed to do.

"You think you can unlock a couple of these speeders?" Colton said, tapping a shiny red one in the row.

"Like steal it?" Abigail said. "That's illegal."

Colton let out a laugh. "We're already running from the police. We just busted out of jail. We're wanted for stealing national treasures. I don't think it matters at this point. And we just need to borrow them. We won't keep them."

Abigail thought for only a second then nodded her head. "Yeah, I think so, but only one. You're horrible at driving, remember?"

That was an unfortunate truth.

Abigail started fumbling with the lock on the red speeder, and either security wasn't all that good or she was really excellent at stuff like this, because in under a minute, the locked popped open.

"You did it!" Colton said.

"Of course I did," Abigail said. "Now come on."

She climbed on first and Colton got on behind her. There was a luggage compartment in the back, and without needing to be told to or anything, Zero hopped right in.

If this dog could seriously understand what they were saying, that was pretty awesome.

Abigail revved up the engine.

"There's an awful lot of controls," she said. "I think because Micronians have four arms. So if I tell you to move a lever or push a button, just do exactly what I say. Nothing else. Okay?"

"Fine, okay," Colton said. "I only pushed a few buttons on the spaceship."

She would never let him live that down.

She placed a hand on either side of the steering controls, and then cranked one.

The speeder launched forward, nearly throwing Colton off the back. There were handles to hold on to, and he grabbed them. Zero didn't seem to be having the same problem. He sat in the luggage compartment, letting his tongue hang from his mouth. Except his tongue was forked, like a snake, not like a dog at all.

81

The speeder was crazy fast, and they were out of the city in minutes, heading across a grassy field toward the river. In the distance, Colton could see hills. Lots and lots of hills. They were too far for him to be able to tell if there were the three hills in a row that they were looking for, but they had to keep going forward.

Colton scanned the horizon for any sign of the Ickians. There was nothing. Actually, there was not much of anything besides the city in the distance. It was like even though the Nebula District was a huge tourist area, nobody ventured far outside of the city. Why did they even come to the planet Micron in the first place? The Micron Meltaways were good, but not good enough to travel across the galaxy for.

Well, maybe once every so often.

"I see the river," Abigail said, motioning with her head. She didn't dare take her hands off the controls. Both their hair was blowing in the wind, making it hard to hear.

"I see it, too," Colton said. "Let's try that area first." He pointed to a clump of hills that were sort of close together. They wouldn't know if it was the right place until they got there, but they had to start somewhere. Also, it felt right. Colton wasn't sure why, but it just did.

"When I tell you to, I'm going to need you to slide the lever—" Abigail said, but Colton couldn't hear the rest of her words over the engine and the wind.

"What?" he said.

"To stop," she said. "When I tell you to, slide the lever—"

Again, her words got drowned out, but he got enough of it this time. She was going to tell him when, and then she wanted him to slide some lever.

"Got it," Colton said.

He looked over her shoulder at the controls. There were three levers, and he was only supposed to slide one of them. But which one? He almost opened his mouth to ask, but shut it. He had this. He could totally figure this out. The lever on the right was already down. The one of the left was really small. But the one in the middle was shiny and clean and looked like it wanted to be slid. That had to be the one.

Almost like the dog could read his mind, Zero let out a bark, confirming his choice. That was all Colton needed.

They sped across the river, hovering less than a foot above the water. Below the surface, Colton could see all sorts of slimy, squirmy things swimming. But their feet weren't even getting wet.

"Get ready!" Abigail said, turning the speeder slightly to the right as they approached the other side of the river.

"Ready," Colton said.

They finished crossing the river.

"Now!" Abigail yelled.

Colton reached forward and slid the lever, all the way to the down position. The good news was that the speeder stopped—immediately. The bad news was that it stopped so fast that they flew off, catapulting through the air, landing twenty yards ahead, face first on the side of a hill.

CHAPTER 13

Colton rolled over and stared up at the sky. Stars flew around in his vision. Except they kept getting closer and closer and then started biting at his face.

These weren't stars! Some kind of alien gnats were nibbling at him. They were as annoying here as they were back on Earth.

Colton swatted them away, and tried to sit up.

"I told you to press the lever SLOWLY!" Abigail said. She lay on her back next to him, and her face was caked with sand. Actually, Colton's was, too. He wiped it off as best as he could.

"I couldn't hear what you said," Colton said. "Just be happy I slid the right lever."

Behind them, totally unfazed by the entire thing, the red speeder hovered in the air. Zero had suffered the same fate as them, but was already up and running around, barking. Colton immediately saw why. Five hills over, Farp and Vomix climbed to the top of a hill. If the Ickians had noticed Colton and Abigail, then weren't showing it.

"Quiet, Zero," Colton said.

The dog immediately stopped barking,

"I think I'm good at training dogs," Colton said.

Abigail smacked him on the shoulder. "This is not a normal dog," she said. "Normal dogs are way hard to train. Trust me, I know. We got two puppies last year, and they are the worst."

Two puppies sounded kind of awesome to Colton. His dad had always told them that they couldn't afford a dog, even though he'd wanted one for as long as he could remember.

"Maybe you're just not very good at it," Colton said.

Abigail only rolled her eyes.

They stood and trudged up the side of the hill, circling around so they were on the side away from Farp and Vomix. The hill was nowhere near as tall as all the stairs they'd had to climb back on Xaxis, but it was made entirely of sand, and Colton's feet kept slipping and sinking so if felt like for every step he took forward he took three steps back. Finally they reached the top.

The very pointy top!

They weren't standing at the top of a hill at all. It was a pyramid, covered by sand so it looked like a hill, but that was only to fool anyone who happened to come looking.

"It is just like the Egyptian pyramids!" Colton said.

"You're right!" Abigail said.

They were exactly where they needed to be.

"Look for a way in," Colton said.

But Zero was already on top of it. He was using his giant paws to dig at the sandy ground. They rushed over just in time for him to uncover a trapdoor in the side of the pyramid.

"This is it!" Abigail said, and the two of them helped the alien dog uncover the rest of the trapdoor. Once they did, Colton yanked on the latch to open it. But it must've been closed for thousands of years, because it didn't budge.

"It's caked with sand," Colton said.

"We can do it together," Abigail said, and the two of them both started pulling on it. Seconds later, it cracked open, revealing the inside of the pyramid—and what looked like a ladder leading down.

"Ready?" Colton said.

Apparently the answer was yes, because Abigail swung a leg over the opening and started down the ladder.

"I hope it holds," she said, and gave out a nervous laugh.

Yeah, if the entire ladder collapsed below them, that would be pretty horrible. Colton grabbed Zero under one arm, because no way was he leaving the little alien dog out here for the Ickians to find. And then he fixed his feet on the ladder and started down.

Whatever the ladder was made of, it seemed to hold, and the darkness didn't turn out to be a problem at all. Every five or ten feet, some kind of automated light turned on when they passed it, lighting up their way. The climb went on way longer that it seemed like it should, which either meant that they were below ground or the pyramid had been built when the ground level had been lower. When they finally touched down at the bottom, all the lights above them went out, but new ones turned on.

They were in an underground chamber, with stone walls and stone blocks for the floor beneath their feet. Dust and cobwebs filled the place, which could only mean one thing: Alien spiders. Colton hoped they weren't giant and huge. Spiders were already something he hated, and the last thing they needed right now were for mutant alien spiders to turn up and eat them.

Fine, so he was letting his imagination get carried away, but if he never saw another spider again, he'd be fine with that.

They took a step forward, and immediately a tunnel lit up ahead of them, almost like an invitation. Zero let out a small whimper but didn't bark.

"I'll lead the way," Colton said.

Abigail whipped around to face him. "Why will you lead the way? You think I can't lead the way since I'm a girl?"

Colton shook his head. "No, nothing like that. I just thought . . . you know . . . in case there are scary spiders or something . . ."

"Scary spiders?" Abigail said, looking at him like he was crazy. "Why scary spiders?"

"Or something like that," Colton said. "Never mind. Let's just go."

They set off down the lighted tunnel, with Zero at their feet. Like the descent down the ladder, it also seemed like they were walking way farther than the length of a single hill.

"I bet all three pyramids are connected underground," Colton said. "And I bet you no one has been down here since they built them."

"How did they stay hidden for so long?" Abigail said. "That doesn't make any sense?"

"Unless the Xaxians did something to help it stay hidden," Colton said. "Like maybe they put some kind of illusion around it."

That seemed like the only way the three pyramids could have gone so long without notice. Or maybe they had been noticed but the Micronians didn't really care.

They walked for a solid ten minutes and finally came to another chamber. But this one only had a single light shining like a spotlight on a stone pedestal. On top of the pedestal rested what had to be the Tablet piece.

"There it is!" Colton said, and he started forward.

Abigail yanked him back. "Don't you know anything about treasure hunting?" she said. "You can't just take off running like that."

91

How was he supposed to know anything about treasure hunting? This was the first official treasure hunt that he'd been on.

"Okay, what do we do?" Colton said, since so far Abigail had proven that she knew what she was doing a lot of the time.

"There are bound to be traps," Abigail said, motioning ahead of them. "You see those blocks that the floor's made of? Step on the wrong one, and you could die."

That was a horrible thought, especially since they'd come this far.

But Zero did not have her same concerns. Before Colton could stop him, the alien dog zipping forward, jumping from one block to the next. He made it to the pedestal, turned, and wagged his weird spiky tail.

"That's the pattern!" Abigail said, pointing at Zero. "Step where he stepped, nowhere else."

She led the way since Colton hadn't kept that good of track of the dog's exact footsteps. But now that he knew it was a matter of life and death, he watched her so closely he almost ran into her three times. But they made it across the floor, and both of them were still alive, so that was good.

The Tablet piece lay there, untouched, on the pedestal. It was a stone sphere, only about a five inches in diameter, and was covered in the same weird symbols and pictures that had been all over the walls back in the temple on Xaxis.

Colton reached for it.

Abigail smacked his hand away.

"Seriously!" she said. "Do you ever listen to a single word I say?"

"What?" he said. "We got through the trap."

"That trap," Abigail said. "But not this one."

Abigail looked upward. Colton's eyes followed her gaze.

Directly overhead the Tablet piece was a solid metal spike, ready to shoot down and destroy anything that disturbed it.

They were completely out of luck.

CHAPTER 14

“This one is the real trap. And there’s no way to get through it,” Abigail said. “If we move the Tablet piece, the spike comes down.”

If Colton’s hand happened to be under it if and when it came down, it would take half his hand off.

“Okay, so what do we do?” Colton asked, placing his hands quickly at his sides.

“Hmmm . . . ,” Abigail said. “It’s probably triggered by weight. If we could put something about the same weight as the Tablet on the pedestal really fast, we could probably trick it.”

"Probably?" Colton said. That didn't sound like good odds.

"Yeah, not the best plan," Abigail said.

"What about the map?" Colton said, holding up the wooden map they'd gotten at the shop back in town. "I could hold this under the spike while you grab the Tablet."

She shook her head. "It'll go right through that. There has to be another way."

Another way. But what? Colton looked around the room, then up at the spike. This was the craziest invention he'd ever seen in his life, put here by aliens trying to protect the Tablet from falling into the wrong hands. But they were the right hands. They needed the Tablet.

Wait, that was it. It was a crazy invention.

"You can do it," Colton said.

Abigail's eyes got wide. "I can do what?"

"You can figure out how it works," Colton said. "Like your other inventions. Or like the cell door back at the jail. Mess with the controls and make it stop."

She seemed to consider this, and then her eyes brightened. "That's a really good idea. Just be ready to run in case I mess things up."

She squatted down and moved around the pedestal, pressing her hands all over it. After five minutes, she stood back up.

"There's no control panel," Abigail said.

"What do you mean?"

"I mean, that I don't know how it works," Abigail said. "I can't find the controls to mess with."

"But we need it," Colton said.

"I know."

The looked around the chamber. The very empty chamber. Then Colton patted his pockets.

Wait! The baseball!

He pulled it from his pocket. "What about this? Will this work?"

Abigail's eyes widened. "That's perfect! That's exactly what we need!"

He handed it to her, but she shook her head.

"You do it," she said. "Inventions and fixing things is what I'm good at, but you're the one who plays sports. You must have quick reflexes."

He could do this. He could totally do this. Colton flexed his fingers. He almost looked upward at the spike one more time, but decided not to. No reason to implant that image in his mind any more than it already was. He took a deep breath and blew it out.

Holding one hand over the Tablet and the other next to it with the baseball, he was ready. Sweat beaded up on his forehead.

Colton grabbed the round stone piece of the Tablet, smoothly, like fielding a ground ball in baseball, and immediately set the baseball in its place, trying to make it one solid motion. Then he yanked his hand back so fast, it was probably faster than light speed.

Okay, bad joke, but he wasn't keeping his hand under the spike 'just to see' what would happen. But nothing bad happened. The spike stayed in place. His baseball sat on the pedestal. And the piece of the Tablet rested in his hands.

He'd done it! But they'd have to celebrate later.

"Let's get out of here," Colton said. He'd find some way to get a new baseball back on Earth.

They turned and jumped from one block to the next, back the way they'd come, Zero leading the way. But no sooner were they out in the lighted tunnel again, they heard voices. Farp and Vomix had found them.

CHAPTER 15

"What are we going to do?" Abigail said. Panic covered her face. They hadn't seen the two Ickians, but their voices echoed down the hallway. They were close.

The tunnel extended in the opposite direction also.

"We run!" Colton said, and they took off down the tunnel, away from Farp and Vomix. He only hoped there was some other way out. Three pyramids hopefully meant three escape routes.

They were in luck! They came to a ladder. Abigail immediately started up. Colton only stopped long enough to grab Zero and then started up himself. When they got to the top, the trapdoor was closed, but Colton handed Zero over to Abigail and used his feet to kick at it as hard as he could.

The trapdoor flew open. They climbed out and closed the trapdoor after them. If they even made it past the traps, Farp and Vomix would find nothing but a baseball. Maybe they'd think that was the treasure they were after.

The speeder was exactly where they left it, and they climbed on, Abigail driving.

"Slowly," Abigail said, and pointed to the lever. "When I tell you to, slide it slowly."

"I got it," Colton said.

Instead of stopping in the city, Abigail circled all the way around. There was no reason to risk running into the guards. Better to go directly to the parking lot, get in their spaceship, and get out of here.

They parked the speeder just outside the parking lot and hurried over toward their spaceship. It was right where they left it, and the door popped open when Colton placed his palm on the panel outside. Programmed for his DNA? That was pretty cool.

Abigail climbed in and Colton followed. Zero sat outside, letting out little barking yips. His antennae sagged sadly.

"Are you coming, boy?" Colton said.

The antennae on Zero's head perked up immediately and his spiky tail went into overdrive, wagging back and forth. He jumped up and down a few times and then hopped into the spaceship, and the door closed behind him. Colton just had time to see the three security guards running their way.

"Take off!" Colton said.

Abigail wasted no time. She pressed whatever buttons she needed to press and slid all the levers and flipped the switches, and the Spaceship Ogre launched off the ground.

"Greetings, Spaceship Ogre," a voice said, coming on over the intercom. "You are requested to land and hand yourself over to officials for immediate imprisonment."

"I don't think so," Abigail said, and she pushed a big yellow button. Spaceship Ogre shot up into the sky, through the clouds, and out of the atmosphere in seconds. She waited only long enough to turn it in the right direction, and then she programmed in the location of Planet Xaxis. Then, with another push of a button, they rocketed forward, vaulting into light speed travel.

They'd done it. They'd found the artifact and gotten away. Sure, they'd been arrested and been chased by evil aliens, but that was ancient history. They'd never have to see the planet Micron again.

Well, unless they wanted to stop back by for a Micron Meltaway.

The stars zipped by them, in long streaks, and their ship moved across the map screen, until finally they dropped out of light speed and Planet Xaxis appeared through the window in front of them.

CHAPTER 16

The ship landed on Xaxis and they jumped out and ran for the temple. Okay, not ran. There had been enough running back on Planet Micron. Maybe walked kind of fast would be a better way to phrase it.

The steps to the top weren't nearly so bad. Or maybe it was just all the excitement pumping through Colton. What a day. What a crazy, cool day.

The second they walked into the temple, the ball of energy in the center began to sizzle. The red and black lightning crackled, and thoughts starting moving into Colton's mind.

Bring the piece of the Tablet forward.

Abigail must've heard it to, because they both walked forward at the same time and stopped in front of the Oracle.

"The Oracle says that you have—" it started.

"Remember?" Colton said. "No 'The Oracle' stuff."

The Oracle paused, then started again.

"You have brought the first piece of the Malevolent and Pure Tablet of Most Epic and Scintillating Power," it said.

"The Tablet," Colton said. "Remember? Just the Tablet."

"Yes, the Tablet," the Oracle said. "Simply the Tablet."

"Did you forget everything while we were gone?" Colton said. "Because I don't want to have to go through this every time."

"It is remembered," the Oracle said. "You simple Earthlings have brought the first piece of the Tablet."

Simple Earthlings! Whatever.

"Right here," Abigail said, holding up the stone sphere.

"Deposit it into the Oracle for collection," the Oracle said.

Into the Oracle? Like how was that supposed to work? From the way the thing sizzled and crackled, it looked like someone could lose a hand if they reached in too far. But to Abigail's credit, she held the Tablet out and lifted it to the ball of energy. Then, she pressed it inside until it disappeared.

The light shifted to blue. Even though it seemed like they should still be able to see the Tablet piece inside it, there was no sign of it. Nothing. It crackled for a few seconds longer, turned back to red and black, and then went silent.

Colton turned to Abigail. "Is that it? Are we supposed to do anything else?"

She shrugged. "I guess not?"

"Then time to head home?" he said, brushing off his hands. It was good to have the whole thing behind them.

"Definitely," Abigail said, and they headed back for the Spaceship Ogre.

CHAPTER 17

It wasn't until the spaceship landed in the junkyard on Earth that Colton actually felt his body relax. Talk about a crazy adventure. Before today, he thought the junkyard dog was the scariest thing he'd run into. Now, the junkyard dog seemed like a silly little puppy.

Oh wait, there were still spiders. They were always going to be scary, no matter what kind of aliens they might run into.

They hopped out of the spaceship and glanced around, looking for Ogre—not the spaceship but the junkyard dog. There was no sign of the giant monster dog so they started for the fence.

"Wait, why are you going that way?" Abigail said when Colton started climbing over.

"How else would I get out of here?" he said.

She motioned with her head, off to the left. "There's a weak spot in the fence down there. You can lift the boards and sneak under."

She led the way, and Colton had to admit that it was way easier than climbing over. Also, climbing over with Zero would have been extra hard. Not impossible. Just hard.

Colton reached over and rubbed Zero's head once they were safely on the other side.

"If I bring you back to my place to live, you'll have to hide from my dad," Colton said. "Do you think you can do that?"

In answer, the alien dog kind of flickered and shifted until it almost blended in with the fence and background behind it.

"No way!" Abigail said. "Your dog can turn invisible. That is the coolest thing ever!"

It was pretty cool, Colton thought. But even cooler was that Zero was his dog. He'd always wanted a dog, and now he had one.

"So what?" Colton said. "We just meet here next time the rings start glowing?" He looked at the ring on his finger. The alien head was blue but not glowing. It looked just like tourist junk. He'd have no trouble explaining where he'd gotten it. People bought these things all over Roswell. He could have found it on the sidewalk. Already he was looking forward to the next time it lit up. Then they could find the second piece of the Tablet.

"Yeah, I guess," Abigail said.

"Okay, well then, I guess I'll see you around," Colton said.

"Yeah, see you around."

Colton and Zero headed away, toward home. But it just seemed so lame. Here, he and Abigail had just saved the galaxy together—or at least started to—and that was the best he could do? That was pathetic.

He turned back. Abigail was just heading away.

"Hey!" Colton called.

She turned around, and Zero let out a happy bark.

"What?" Abigail said.

"You know, if you ever want to hang out before then, we could always do that," Colton said. He wasn't sure what they'd do. Maybe she would want to throw the baseball. Or she could show him some of that cool invention stuff she did. Whatever. It didn't really matter.

"That would be cool," Abigail said, shrugging like maybe she didn't think it was that big of a deal.

"But not at my house," Colton said. "My dad doesn't really like visitors."

"That's no problem," Abigail said. "I live just over on Aztec Road. White two-story house. You can't miss it. And my parents love visitors. Come by anytime."

"Perfect!" Colton said.

"But . . ."

"But what?"

"But you have to bring Zero," Abigail said. "My puppies will love him. No Zero. No visit."

Colton couldn't help the grin that crept onto his face. "That is not a problem at all."

He was about to turn away when they heard hammering. Down the fence, about twenty yards away, some guy in a ball cap was tacking a sign to the fence of the junkyard.

"Is that Crazy Joe?" Colton said.

Crazy Joe was a local legend in Roswell. Rumors had it that he'd been abducted by aliens. The rumors claimed he'd been taken to the future by the aliens, and barely escaped being eaten by monsters.

109

"I think so," Abigail said, rubbing her eyes.

"What do you think the signs say?" Colton said.

"Let's go find out," Abigail said, starting toward it.

"The end is coming!" Crazy Joe shouted when he spotted them. "Beware! The end is coming!"

Then he moved further down the fence to tack up another sign. His smell lingered though, because if his appearance could be believed, he hadn't taken a shower in years.

"And that's why they call him crazy," Colton said.

"Uh oh," Abigail said, pointing to the sign.

Roswell Junkyard
to be flattened
and removed on

June 15th

to make way for
Movie Theater.

"Flattened and removed!" Colton said. "They can't do that."

"But they are," Abigail said. "I heard rumors that they were putting in a new movie theater, but I had no idea it was going to be here. This is horrible!"

"So what do we do?" Colton said. "We can't let it happen. We need the junkyard. We need the spaceship. And this only gives us one week. One week!"

This was the worst. Just when summer was looking up, some movie theater company was going to come in and destroy their spaceship? How were they supposed to save the galaxy with no spaceship?

"We'll find a way to stop it," Abigail said.

"How?"

"I don't know," she said. "But I bet we can figure it out together."

They better. Or else the galaxy was going to be in serious trouble.

A NOTE FROM CONNOR

To all the Space Travelers out there:

Thank you so much for taking the time to read *Alien Treasure Hunters*! It's adventurers (and readers) like you who will save the future!

If you did enjoy reading *Alien Treasure Hunters*, I would love if you would take a few moments to review the book on Amazon. Reviews are so important these days, and even a one sentence review can make a huge difference in other readers discovering the series.

Now go and save the galaxy
(or read another book)!

—CONNOR HOOVER

LOOKING FOR MORE
**ALIEN
TREASURE
HUNTERS?**

THE ADVENTURE
CONTINUES IN

**ALIEN
TREASURE
HUNTERS
BOOK 2!**

LIKE VIDEO GAMES?
THINK MAGIC AND MONSTERS
ARE COOL?

LOOK FOR

A SERIES BY
CONNOR HOOVER!

SIGN UP FOR THE
LATEST NEWS HERE:

www.connorhoover.com

LOOK FOR

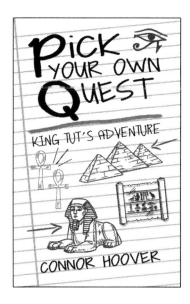

Ancient Egypt is in serious trouble…

Crazy things are happening in Egypt! The gods are angry. The Nile River is drying up. Smoke appears on the horizon. Crocodiles attack! It's up to you to save the world. Make the right choice and you get to rule Egypt for the rest of your life. Make the wrong choice and it will be your last.

Remember, you can't turn back. Sorry! Once you make a choice, it can't be changed.

CHOOSE WISELY :)

ABOUT THE AUTHOR

Connor Hoover wanted to be an astronaut and to travel to other galaxies, but when that didn't work out, Connor wrote about space-traveling treasure hunters instead. It's actually pretty fun.

To contact Connor:

connor@connorhoover.com

www.connorhoover.com

Made in the USA
Lexington, KY
19 February 2018